Mindful Bea
and the WORRY TREE

by Gail Silver
illustrated by Franziska Höllbacher

FOR ANABEL. MAY EVERY BIRTHDAY BE YOUR VERY BEST—GS

FOR MOM AND DAD. THANKS FOR EVERYTHING—FH

Magination Press

Books for Kids from the
American Psychological Association.

maginationpress.org

Magination Press is a registered trademark of the American Psychological Association.
Order books here: www.apa.org/pubs/magination or 1-800-374-2721

Book design by Sandra Kimbell
Printed by Worzalla, Stevens Point, WI

Library of Congress Cataloging-in-Publication Data

Names: Silver, Gail, author. | Hollbacher, Franziska, illustrator.
Title: Mindful Bea and the worry tree / by Gail Silver ; illustrated by Franziska Hollbacher.
Description: Washington, DC : Magination Press, [2019] | "American Psychological Association." |
  Summary: Bea anxiously awaits her birthday party guests, worrying about all the things that could
  go wrong, until her mother reminds her that deep breathing will help her relax.
  Includes note to parents.
Identifiers: LCCN 2018011909| ISBN 9781433829543 (hardcover) | ISBN 1433829541 (hardcover)
Subjects: | CYAC: Worry--Fiction. | Birthdays—Fiction. | Parties—Fiction.
Classification: LCC PZ7.S58567 Min 2019 |
  DDC [E]—dc23 LC record available at
  https://lccn.loc.gov/2018011909

Manufactured in the United States of America
10 9 8 7 6 5 4 3 2 1

Bea lives here, in this house with its yard and wide willow tree that towers and sways and bends in the breeze.

Bea climbs and swings, and dances and sings, and when she's inspired (and not too tired), makes make-believe towns from twigs and things she finds on the ground.

But today, the swing is still. The air untouched.
Twigs and things are strewn around.
There's no singing or dancing. Today there's no sound.

Except for the one from inside the home.
It's a soft and steady, whimpering groan.

If you look through the window, you can see Bea.
She's curled up in bed with a case of—well, come and see.

"It's time for your party," Bea's mother says.
Bea moans and quivers and shakes her head.

"What's wrong?" Mama asks, though she already knows.
She's seen before how this thing grows—on Bea's skin and in her hair.
Soon it will be everywhere.

Like a seed from underground,
it sprouts alive, unleashed, unbound.

With gnarled roots, this kind of tree feeds
on thoughts...

"IT'S MY **ANXieTy**," sighs Bea.
She lifts her head and worry peaks.
Worry springs. Worry speaks.

Bea's stomach flips.
It flops. It flutters.

Through the hall, with heavy feet...
gnarled roots, knotty tree...

A billion butterflies on overdrive circle up as friends arrive.

I'm not ready yet to see my friends.

Worry calls, beats, and hammers.
"What if, what if?" worry clamors.

"WHAT IF? WHAT IF..."

...the air is cool.

"WHAT IF? WHAT IF..."

...the sky is wide.

"WHAT IF? WHAT IF..."

...birds sing from someplace high.

"What if? What if?"
Bea thinks,

What if...
I try...

Just one breath in,
then one breath out.

One breath in, one breath out.

Another in, slow and long—

—a light, airy rhythm song.

Breathing in, breathing out.

DING DONG! And the sound of friends, not far away.
"Let's wait for the others,"
Bea hears one say.

Hwooo-Haaahhh

One more breath.
I'll stand up soon.

Hwoo—HaaahhhmyGosh!
We forgot the balloons!

Flip and flutter, slip and stutter.
Open bag, spray of rubber.

Orange, yellow,
blue, green, red—

A deep one in,
slow and long.
Listen for the rhythm song.

Hwooo-Haaahhh

DING DONG!

Both eyes closed,
she takes another.

Filled with breath,
she hears her mother.
"Come on, kids. Bea's out back."

Bea breathes in.
        Slow
         Slow
      Slow
     Slow

Filled with breath,
She lets it
   Go
      Go
        Go
          Go

Bea breathes in.
        Slow
         Slow
      Slow
     Slow

Filled with breath,
She lets it
   Go
      Go
        Go
          Go

The string is tied,
Bea's arm's raised high.
A warm wind is passing by.

Friends at the ready,
race through the gate—
steady now—it's time to celebrate.

Arms linked—laughter abounds.
Mama sighs,

Relief resounds.

There are streamers and treats,
and games to play, and in the sky
a song in blue that slipped away.

Above the tree a blue balloon,
a rhythm song sung by Bea.

Note to Parents & Caregivers

by Ara J. Schmitt, PhD

Worry, or anxiety, is a normal emotional reaction to something dangerous in our environment. In fact, anxiety helps us avoid something that is likely to cause us harm. For example, the anxiety that results from hearing a rattle-like sound on a hiking trail may help us avoid an encounter with a rattle snake. However, children may be prone to *excessive* worry and worry about events that are *unlikely* to happen (like Bea). When such anxiety negatively impacts a child's everyday life, a mental health professional may diagnose the presence of an anxiety disorder. Approximately 15-20% of children in the United States are believed to meet criteria for an anxiety disorder across their childhood. At the root of anxiety-related disorders are worry thoughts.

How to Use This Book

Mindful Bea and the Worry Tree is a useful book for any child that frequently experiences excessive worry. Bea is over-taken by worry regarding her upcoming birthday party. She engages in a series of worry thoughts, or what psychologists call "cognitive distortions." These result in her having labored breathing, an upset stomach, and even not wanting to go to her own party! Bea ultimately decides that she will take control of her worry thoughts and breathing. She ends up enjoying her party and is able to work through a small mishap—forgetting to blow up balloons. Parents of children with excessive worry might use this book to discuss Bea's worries and how those negative thoughts impacted Bea.

Then, parents can talk with their child about the worry thoughts they are experiencing and how those thoughts negatively impact their life at home and school. Using the guidance below, parents might gently confront their child's worry thoughts and teach their child to engage in a simple relaxation exercise to overcome excessive worry.

Understanding Bea's Worry Thoughts

Children display many of the same worry thoughts as adults. Bea showed us at least five types of worry thoughts. The first worry thought is a form of *must* or *should thinking.* Although Bea does not make such statements directly, she appears to believe that her birthday party must be flawless; her party should be perfect and, if not, her guests will not enjoy themselves. This leads Bea to engage in the second distortion, *black-or-white thinking.* Bea appears to believe that her party will either be perfect and everyone will have fun, or the party will be disastrous with unhappy guests. There is no room for middle ground. In her mind, it does not seem possible to have a disappointing hiccup along the way, but still a great party overall. As a result of these unreasonable thoughts, Bea appears to *jump to conclusions.* She seems certain that any mistake at the party will upset her friends and this could result in her friends calling her names, or not wanting to stay at the party.

The worry thought Bea appears to have most often is called *catastrophizing.* This fourth worry thought shows that a child expects negative events to happen. We know this because Bea repeatedly

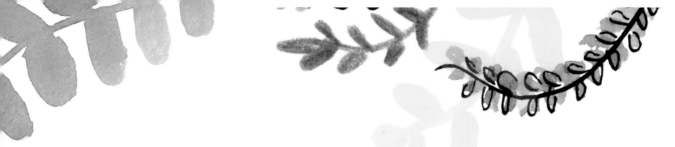

asks "what if?" questions. What if there isn't enough cake? What if no one shows up? What if the piñata doesn't break? None of these are likely to happen, yet Bea worries about every possible poor outcome. Finally, Bea is able to catastrophize because she engages in a fifth worry thought, *filtering.* She filters out all positive thoughts and evidence that the party will go well (e.g., current preparation by her mother and experience of past birthday parties) in favor of negative thoughts.

How Parents Can Help

Parents can explain that the body and mind are connected, and calming the body can help to calm the mind. The worries can still be there for now, but they can use their breath to help their body feel better. During the tense moments of worry thoughts, parents can lead their child through this simple relaxation exercise. Although a variety of methods exist that also involve tensing muscles, the following exercise is a simple four-step breathing routine that can be used in virtually any location, including school.

1. In a calm, reassuring voice, prompt your child to put a pause on their worry thoughts. It can help to give them a concrete suggestion, such as telling their worries directly that they have something else they need to do for a minute, or picturing a stop sign to signal a pause. Then, help them bring their attention to their breath.

2. Next, ask your child to take in a long breath through their nose until their lungs are full.

3. Then, have your child hold their breath for a short time. To the count of three will do.

4. Finally, tell your child to exhale slowly through their mouth like they are blowing out a candle.

These steps can be repeated as necessary to reduce worry that is causing negative physical symptoms.

It's useful for children to practice this exercise when worry is not present, as well, so that it is easier for them to switch their thoughts and attention when they are dealing with anxiety.

Parents can also take steps to prevent excessive worry thoughts from taking hold. Parents should be prepared to gently challenge worry thoughts and reinforce positive, realistic thoughts. To do this, parents can use the child's previous experiences, or even talk through their own personal experiences with worry thoughts.

To counteract *must/should thinking,* parents might reinforce that all one can do is prepare as well as possible and then do their best. Reinforce that successes and disappointments are part of life. *Black-or-white thinking* can be challenged by asking the child to think of instances, or sharing instances, where there were positive and negative aspects to an event, like a recent family vacation. The child must recognize that persons, places, and events all have positive and negative aspects. *Jumping to conclusions* and *catastrophizing* may be challenged through a similar technique. In short, these two worry thoughts involve a child forecasting that something negative will happen. Parents might prompt the worried child to list all of the negative thoughts that are troubling them. Then, the parent could lead the child through a discussion of how likely those things are to happen, and for those that could reasonably occur, what might be done in response. Chances are, very few of the worries are likely to come true, and for those that might, a simple solution exists that will limit any lasting negative consequences. Finally, *filtering* as a worry thought pattern may also be counteracted using the listing technique. In addition to listing worries, a child might be prompted to list positive aspects of a person, place, or event to reinforce there is reason for optimism. Further, if worry thoughts have taken hold, a parent might lead the child through a list of facts that disconfirm the worry thought or suggest the worry will not actually come true. With a list of positive aspects and evidence that suggests the negative event won't happen, a parent can point out to the child that they seem to focus on negative thoughts and ignore positive evidence and thoughts.

WHEN TO SEEK PROFESSIONAL HELP

Parents often struggle to know when to seek the assistance of a mental health professional. If the focus of worry does not seem typical for a child that age, or if the worry is intensifying and spreading, the assistance of a professional is encouraged. Further, seek help if a child conveys hopelessness that their worry will never get better, or if a child expresses thoughts of self-harm. Disturbed sleep, panic attacks, unusual crying and clinging, persistent nightmares, bedwetting, and extreme avoidance of anxiety-provoking stimuli are also signs that professional intervention may be in order. In sum, parents are the experts of their child and know their child best. If excessive worry is disrupting your child's life, seek assistance.

Ara J. Schmitt, PhD, is an associate professor of school psychology at Duquesne University. His primary research interests involve the neuropsychological assessment and intervention of learning problems and pediatric disorders. Dr. Schmitt is also a licensed psychologist and certified school psychologist.

ABOUT THE AUTHOR

Gail Silver is the author of the award-winning *Anh's Anger, Steps and Stones,* and *Peace, Bugs, and Understanding.* Gail is also a feature writer for *Lions Roar Magazine* and co-writer of the animated screenplay, *Planting Seeds: The Power of Mindfulness.* She is director of Yoga Child, Inc., and founder and CEO of The School Mindfulness Project, Inc., a non-profit organization providing sustainable mind-body education to underserved Philadelphia schools. Gail lives in Philadelphia, Pennsylvania, with her family. Visit @GailPSilver on Twitter and gailsilverbooks.com.

ABOUT THE ILLUSTRATOR

Franziska Höllbacher has loved art and drawing since she was a little girl. She has been illustrating children's books for both national and international publishers for three years now. She currently studies multimedia Art in Salzburg, Austria. Visit @franzi_illustrates on Instagram, @franzi_illus on Twitter, and at franzi-illustrates.com.

ABOUT MAGINATION PRESS

Magination Press is the children's book imprint of the American Psychological Association, the largest scientific and professional organization representing psychologists in the United States and the largest association of psychologists worldwide. Visit maginationpress.org.